This igloo book belongs to:

....

Contents

igloobooks

Published in 2014
by Igloo Books Ltd
Cottage Farm
Sywell
NN6 0BJ
www.igloobooks.com

FIR003 0814
12 14 15 13 11
ISBN: 978-0-85734-496-0

Printed and manufactured in China

Illustrated by Mike Garton
Stories by Melanie Joyce

Stories
for 4
Year
Olds

igloobooks

Walter to the Rescue

Walter the giraffe was playing at the park with his friends. But, he wasn't very happy.

"What's the matter, Walter?" asked Josh.

"You're all having loads of fun," said Walter. "But, I'm too big for the climbing frame, I'm not having any fun at all."

"Why don't you have a go on the slide?" said Sammy.
But, when Walter got onto the slide, his long legs nearly reached
the bottom. "You see?" said Walter, feeling very annoyed, "I'm just
too big to have fun."

5

"Let's play chase," said Josh. But, Walter's friends were very quick and whizzed round and round. Walter couldn't turn his long legs that quickly and he soon got caught. "It's no fun being me," he said, hanging his head.

6

Suddenly, there was a loud cry, "Help, help!" said a voice.
"I'm stuck!" It was Walter's friend, Elly. She had climbed right up to
the top of the climbing frame, but now she was too frightened to
climb back down.

Walter quickly went over on his long, graceful legs. "Don't worry, Elly," he said. "Climb onto my neck and I'll lower you down."

So, Elly climbed onto Walter's neck and she was soon safely on the ground. Everyone cheered and said, "Hooray for Walter!"

"Thank you for rescuing me, Walter," said Elly "It's a good job you've got long legs and a long neck."

Walter felt shy and he went a bit red. "Maybe it's not so bad being me after all," he said.

Charlie's Big Dig

One day, Charlie invited his friend, Roly, round to play. "Make sure you don't get up to any mischief," said Mum.

"We won't," said Charlie and Roly, as they ran off outside to see what interesting things they could find to do.

"I wish we had some swings, or a slide to play on," said Charlie.
Just then, there was the sound of shuffling and giggling coming
from next door.
"You go first," said a voice. "No, you go first," said another.
Suddenly, a small furry head bounced right up above the fence.

11

A few minutes later, another furry head bounced up and down. Charlie and Roly tried to jump up, to see who it was, but the fence was too high. No matter how hard they tried, they couldn't jump high enough to see over it.

12

"I want to find out who's bouncing next door," said Charlie.
"Me, too," added Roly.
So, they sniffed around at the bottom of the fence and then they began to dig. Charlie dug a bit, then Roly dug a bit. Soon, there was a hole just big enough for Charlie to poke his head through.

In next door's garden, there was a trampoline and bouncing up and down on it were Daisy and her friend, Jane. They looked like they were having loads of fun. "Hello," they giggled. "Would you like to come and play on our trampoline?"
"Yes, please," said Charlie.

But, when Charlie tried to pull his head out from under the fence, it wouldn't move. "I'm stuck!" he said to Roly. So, Roly pulled and tugged and heaved, but he couldn't get Charlie free.

Luckily, Mum was watching from the kitchen window. "I knew you two would get up to mischief," she said, coming outside.

Mum dug and dug and soon, Charlie was free. "Next time, if you
need help with something, remember to ask," said Mum, gently.
"Sorry," said Charlie. "Sorry," said Roly. Then they started to fill in
the hole.

When the soil was all nice and smooth, Mum took Charlie and
Roly next door to play. They had lots of fun, jumping and bouncing
on the big trampoline with their new friends, Daisy and Jane. Best
of all, Mum was there to make sure there was no more mischief.

17

Heather and the Weather

Heather didn't like the weather. "It keeps changing," she said. On Monday and Tuesday, it was sunny and light, so Heather pulled on her best, red swimsuit and splashed about in the little paddling pool. "I love the sunshine!" she cried.

18

On Wednesday, clouds pushed in front of the sun and the sky was moody and grey. "I'll have to wear my jumper and my old red jeans, now," said Heather. She wasn't happy, so she scowled and frowned.

On Thursday, the rain fell in blobs and splats. Heather wore her yellow rain coat and her flowery rain hat. But, the rain hat leaked and Heather got wet. She ran inside and looked out of the window. "I don't like the rain," she complained.

On Friday, the sun peeped out. "I can play on the slide," Heather cried. So, Heather put on her best spotty top and her pretty, pink shorts. But the sun disappeared and the sky grew dark and very, very quiet. "I don't like this," said Heather, and she ran inside.

21

On Saturday, black clouds gathered. "Go away clouds, I want to play," shouted Heather and she shook her fist. But, the sky rumbled and grumbled. Lightning crackled and flashed. "I don't like storms," said Heather and she quivered and shivered and ran inside.

On Sunday, the sun came out and Heather was happy. "You're a bit like the weather," said Mum. "Sometimes you're clouds and rain and, very occasionally, you're thunder and lightning. But mostly, you're like soft, summer sunshine."

Heather smiled at her mum. "I like the weather," she said.

The Big, Toy Shop

Elsie's Teddy was very, very old. "I think it's time we let Old Teddy have a rest," said Mum. "Let's go to the toy shop and you can choose a brand new one."

So, Elsie and her mum went off to the big toy shop.

Inside the shop, there were lots of teddy bears. Elsie didn't know which one to choose. Then, suddenly, she heard a voice say, "Hello." It was Elsie's friend, Tom, and he had come to look at the teddy bears, too.

"The stuffing has all come out of my teddy," said Tom, showing it to Elsie. "Mummy says I can have a new one. We could look together." So, Elsie and Tom went to look at the teddy bears while their mums had a chat.

26

All the teddies were neatly displayed, but there was one little bear sitting all on his own. He wore a bright blue jacket with red, patterned trousers, a little felt hat and small, furry boots.
"He's lovely," said Elsie. "He's cute," said Tom.

27

They looked at their mums and they looked at the little teddy. Then, at the same time, Tom and Elsie both said, "I want this one!" Elsie took one arm and Tom took the other and they both began to pull. "He's mine," said Tom.
"No, he's mine," said Elsie.

28

They pulled the teddy this way and that.
"I want him!" said Elsie and she pulled at the little teddy's hat.
"No, I want him!" said Tom and he tugged at the teddy's boot.
Then, suddenly, the hat came off and a boot came loose.

Tom toppled backwards and fell on the floor and Elsie landed with a bump, on her bottom. "Ouch!" they both said, looking very surprised. Their mums looked very surprised, too. "It's not nice to squabble," they said.

Just then, the shop assistant came over holding another teddy, just like the other one. "Here you are," she said. "There's no need to argue. Now you can have a teddy each."

Elsie and Tom felt silly for squabbling. But, they were very glad they had new teddies to cuddle.

Alice's Surprise

Alice and her friends, Pip and Max, were dressing up for Halloween.
"I'm going to be a witch," said Pip, pulling on a tall, black hat.
"I'm going to be a wizard," said Alice, waving a sparkly wand.

"I'm going to be a ghost with rattling chains," said Max and he pulled on a sheet with holes for eyes.

Suddenly, there was a noise on the stairs. It was a chinking, clinking, clanging sort of noise and it was coming closer.

33

"What is it?" asked Pip.
"It sounds like chains clanking," replied Alice.
"What if it's a real ghost?" whispered Max.

At the top of the stairs, the strange noise stopped. Suddenly, there was a bump against the bedroom door.

34

Alice screamed. Pip screamed. Max screamed, too!
Pip dived under the bed. Alice jumped into the dressing-up box and
Max hid in the wardrobe.

Very slowly, the door began to open and a clinking, clanging
shape came in.

Alice stared. Pip stared. Max stared, too! Alice thought the shadow looked very familiar. Then, a big, deep voice boomed, "Where is everyone? I've brought you some lemonade and cookies." It was Alice's dad. "We thought you were a ghost," said Alice.

"No," laughed Dad. "It was just the glasses chinking, as I walked up the stairs. Come on, you lot, I think you need a drink and a cookie after all that excitement."

So, they all had lemonade, cookies and a very spooky, Halloween.

Nigel's Brush

It was painting day at Nigel's house. Mum put a new sheet of paper on the easel. Nigel got out his paints, his blue dungarees and his big, special brush. "Let's mix some paints," said Mum.
"Not too runny and not too thick."

Nigel smiled and picked up his brush. He was just about to dip it into some paint when, *drring, drring*, the telephone rang. "Wait a minute, Nigel," said Mum and she went into the hall.

But, Nigel didn't want to wait. With a gloop and a splosh he dipped his big, special brush into a pot of pink paint and went SPLODGE, onto the clean, white paper.

"It's fun!" said Nigel, swishing his brush. Then, he cleaned it in a glass of water and dipped it into another pot of paint.

Nigel giggled and splashed and splatted all the bright paints in his big, paint tray.

Then, *click*, went the phone in the hallway and Mum came
back in. She looked at Nigel and she looked at the picture.
Her eyes grew wide and her mouth grew wider. "Nigel!" she cried.
"I told you to wait. You're covered in paint!"

"I drew a picture of you, Mummy," said Nigel, with a smile.
Mum sighed and then she smiled, too. "Thank you, Nigel," she said.
"That's very kind of you. But I think we need to go upstairs
and get you cleaned up."

Mum took Nigel upstairs. "Take off those dirty dungarees," she said, "and jump into this nice, soapy bath."
"If it rains, can we do painting tomorrow, Mummy?" asked Nigel.
"Yes, Nigel," said Mum, "but next time, we'll do it together!"

43

Mum Says, "Goodnight"

Bradley was looking at his new space monster book.
"Are there really monsters in space?" he asked Mum.
"No, there's no such thing," said Mum, gently. "Come on now,
it's bedtime. You go upstairs and I'll come and tuck you in."

So, Bradley ran upstairs, brushed his teeth and put on his soft, stripy pyjamas. Then, he jumped into bed and waited for Mum to come and tuck him in. Bradley waited and waited, but Mum didn't come.

The wind blew clouds across the moon and rattled Bradley's window.
He looked outside at the shadows and shapes. "What if space monsters
really do exist?" whispered Bradley. "What if they come from the
moon, into my room?"

46

Just then, Bradley heard a shuffle on the stairs and saw
a shadow stretch up over the banister and along the wall.
"Is that you, Mum?" whispered Bradley, in a small, scared voice.
But no one answered. So, Bradley sunk right down and pulled his quilt
up to his chin. "Are you a space monster?" he called out, bravely.

"No, Bradley," said a soft, laughing voice. "It's me, Mummy and I've come to tuck you in, kiss you goodnight and tell you a story. But not one about space monsters!"

Bradley was very relieved. He still loved space monsters, but he was glad that they only existed in books.

48